All rights reserved. Published in the United States by Random House Children's Books, a division of Penguin Random House LLC, 1745 Broadway, New York, NY 10019, and in Canada by Penguin Random House Canada Limited, Toronto.

randomhousekids.com
dcsuperherogirls.com
dckids.com

ISBN 978-1-524-70106-2 (trade)
ISBN 978-1-524-70107-9 (ebook)

Printed in the United States of America
10 9 8 7 6 5 4 3 2 1

SUPER HERO HIGH SCHOOL YEARBOOK

By Shea Fontana

Random House 🏠 New York

Super Hero High School

Welcome to Super Hero High

I was honored when I was asked to write the introduction to this year's Super Hero High School yearbook. During my time covering the Super Hero High news, I've gotten to know the students, and they are some of the most capable, skilled, and downright powerful supers-in-training in the entire universe. It's here that students discover their unique abilities, develop their powers, and master the fundamentals of being a super hero.

And it's that last part that's really important. Super Hero High accepts all kinds of supers. Some students, like Wonder Woman, are born with their powers, and others, such as Bumblebee and Cyborg, get their powers from technological inventions. Then there are students like Batgirl who use only their smarts, skills, and determination to make themselves super. But no matter what powers a student has, Super Hero High helps them unlock

their full potential and become the best they can be. The teachers at SHHS believe anyone can be a hero—because anyone can!

Super Hero High offers its students a great environment in which to reach the apex of their abilities. There's a wide range of classes, including Weaponomics, Flyers' Ed, Heroes Throughout History, and my favorite, Super Suit Design, where students design high-tech wear to aid them on their missions. In addition to these classes, there are extracurricular activities, such as the Science Club, Junior Detective Society, and even sports like Heroball for burning off that extra-super energy.

And of course, the Hero of the Month awards put the spotlight on students who have really shined. These exemplary students deserve recognition not only for saving Metropolis from invading aliens, rampaging giants, and crazed super-villains, but also for their hard work, kindness, and commitment to teamwork.

So get your cape on and celebrate another great year at Super Hero High!

Always on the scene,

Lois Lane

Ace reporter and future Pulitzer Prize winner

WONDER WOMAN

Wonder Woman grew up on the island of Themyscira, which was populated with female warriors. As Princess of Themyscira, she's a natural-born leader, and it's her mission to make the entire universe a better place. She chose to attend Super Hero High with the goal of becoming the greatest hero she can be!

Place of Origin:	Themyscira
Powers and Skills:	Super-strength, super-speed, flight
Specialty:	Deflecting lasers, bullets, and projectiles of all types with her unbreakable bracelets
Weapons:	The magic Lasso of Truth, indestructible bracelets, and a shield of Themysciran steel
Favorite Food:	Sugary cereals—the more colorful, the better!
Fashion Sense:	Athletic and practical

Oh my Hero —
I loved playing Heroball with you!
See you at the Model United Planets
meet! Wonder Woman

SUPERGIRL

spacey and totally out there

Supergirl is a new ∧ student from the planet Krypton. She's the most powerful teen at Super Hero High . . . and on Earth! She might be a little clumsy while she learns to control all her amazing powers, but she never gives up.

Place of Origin: The planet Krypton

Powers and Skills: Super-strength; super-speed; flight; invulnerability; super-cold breath; and X-ray, telescopic, microscopic, and heat vision

Specialty: Saving the day, being a super friend

Favorite Food: Superfood Cake

Fashion Sense: Peppy and preppy

STAY SUPER!
— SUPERGIRL

BATGIRL

Batgirl is an off-the-charts, just-forget-about-the-test super genius. Her greatest power is her brainpower! As a student, Batgirl is completely confident, cool, and collected. When she's not honing her detective skills, she's inventing high-tech gadgets, building new Bat-bunkers, and making communication bracelets for all her friends.

Place of Origin:	Gotham City
Powers and Skills:	Advanced deduction and crime-fighting skills, computer and technological genius, martial arts
Specialty:	Keeping her cool in any situation, making mods to her Batjet
Favorite Food:	Superfood Cake (if Supergirl doesn't eat it all first!)
Fashion Sense:	Sleek, dark, practical, and tech-y

POW! yearbook on! Batgirl

HARLEY QUINN

She's unorganized and unpredictable but tons of fun! She's the jokester girl who just wants to have ~~fun~~ *FUUUN!* As the resident class clown, Harley captures her classmates' best—and worst—moments for her Web channel, "Harley's Quintessentials."

WHO, ME

REALLY, REALLY, POPULAR

YOU CAN ALSO CALL ME...
✓ THE HARLSTER
✗ SUPERSTAR ✗
✓ THE GIRL EVERYBODY WANTS TO BE LIKE
✓ GOTHAM CITY'S GREATEST COMEDIC GENIUS

Place of Origin: Gotham City

Powers and Skills: Acrobatics, unpredictability, keen sense of humor

Weapon: A very large mallet

Specialty: Finding the funny

Favorite Food: Kaboom Candy Cupcakes

Fashion Sense: Colorful, wacky

★ BOLD ★ INCREDIBLE ★ AWESOME
★ ATTENTION-GRABBING ★ FASHION FORWARD

GOTCHA!!!

BUMBLEBEE

Bumblebee is the ultimate fly on the wall! She's an upbeat engineering genius, and the high-tech suit she built allows her to fly, shrink, and blast shocking bee stings! Her shrinking skills get her into places no other Super can access. Beyond her save-the-day savvy, she also brings the best beats and cape-shaking music as the class DJ.

Place of Origin:	Metropolis
Powers and Skills:	Ability to shrink to the size of a bee, flight, super-strength in shrunken form
Weapon:	Blasters that emit electric stings
Specialty:	Extreme stealth, pulling off the best surprise parties
Favorite Food:	Honey-flavored anything
Fashion Sense:	Stylish with a hint of tech

Here's the Buzz—
You Rock!
XOXO Bumblebee

POISON IVY

Poison Ivy is a bit on the shy side—in fact, she's more comfortable with plants than people—but she's finally starting to blossom. Ever since a lab accident gave her incredible abilities with the plant kingdom, she's been quietly searching for ways to increase her superpowers so she can grow from a small acorn into a mighty oak!

Place of Origin:	Gotham City
Powers and Skills:	Ability to control plants and accelerate plant growth, biology genius
Specialty:	Green thumb
Favorite Food:	Bacon and eggs—anything but salad!
Fashion Sense:	Green and earthy

Sorry! Chompy ate your bio homework . . . and your shoes . . . and your locker . . .
— Poison Ivy

KATANA

Katana wields her sword with skill, style, and grace! She has traveled around the world and is always on the cutting edge of fashion. She's fearless and uber funky. When she's not fighting crime, Katana is sharpening her skills as a designer and an artist.

Katana's award-winning painting from the Super Hero High Student Art Show fund-raiser.

Place of Origin:	Japan
Powers and Skills:	Martial arts, sword fighting, and the ability to make a weapon out of just about anything
Weapons:	Sword, throwing stars
Specialty:	Fighting crime with style!
Favorite Food:	Chopped salad
Fashion Sense:	Cutting-edge couture

STAY SHARP!!!
— KATANA

CATWOMAN

Catwoman is one feisty feline! She grew up an orphan in Gotham City, so she's fiercely independent and loves to bend the rules. Insatiably curious, she can't help trying to crack locks and computer codes, and slips past security systems just for fun.

Place of Origin:	Gotham City
Powers and Skills:	Agility, speed, quick reflexes, gymnastics, and stealth
Specialty:	Getting away with it . . . whatever it is!
Favorite Food:	Sushi
Fashion Sense:	Sleek and black

Have a great year, kitten!

23

CHEETAH

Cheetah considers herself superior to her classmates at Super Hero High. She's *purr*-fectly willing to use her claws to get what she wants, especially the attention and praise she thinks she deserves. Cheetah is one of Super Hero High's most competitive students. Her determination makes her a star on the Heroball field, and there's nothing she won't do to win.

Place of Origin:	Nottingham~~shire, England~~ *None of your business*
Powers and Skills:	Agility, speed, sharp reflexes, *I.E: stay out of my way!* and even sharper claws
Specialty:	Quick strikes, ~~Ice~~ *CLASSIFIED*
Favorite Food:	Lamb kebabs
Fashion Sense:	Athletic and amazing

HAWKGIRL

With her wide wingspan and warrior spirit, Hawkgirl has an honorable sense of good and evil and stands up to fight for what's right. As the hall monitor of Super Hero High, she takes pride in always following the rules and holds her friends to the same standards. Hawkgirl also has a passion for history and a keen interest in ancient artifacts and weaponry. Her days are highly regimented, but that doesn't mean she can't have fun . . . it just has to be scheduled!

Place of Origin:	St. Roch
Powers and Skills:	Flight, multiple fighting styles, detection, and sleuthing
Weapons:	Mace, gravity-defying Nth Metal belt and harness
Favorite Food:	Gummy worms
Fashion Sense:	Vintage vogue

I hope your dreams come true.
(Unless you dream of breaking the rules.
Then I'll have to give you detention.)
Sinceramente, Hawkgirl

STAR SAPPHIRE

The school's top diva, Star Sapphire gets her abilities from the power ring she wears. Not only does her ring grant her the ability to create violet energy constructs, it also gives her unique powers over love and allows her to influence other people's emotions—which can cause harmony or heartbreak, depending on the mood she's in.

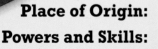

Place of Origin:	Coast City
Powers and Skills:	Flight; the ability to create hard light constructs, force fields, and violet energy blasts
Weapon:	Star Sapphire power ring
Specialty:	Star Sapphire's power ring allows her to affect the emotion of love in others . . . and that causes more trouble than you might think!
Favorite Foods:	Plums, eggplants, and grapes
Fashion Sense:	Shades of violet and magenta

Love ya!
Star Sapphire

The students of Super Hero High would like to thank Star Sapphire's parents and the Ferris Air Company for their generous donation, which allowed us to rebuild the cafeteria after Supergirl's most recent accident.

BEAST BOY

Beast Boy can change into any animal he wants, anytime he wants (well, most of the time). He's known to be happy-go-lucky and a little immature, but when the situation gets serious, you want this animal on your side. He's a loyal friend who's just as comfortable hanging out with the girls as he is goofing off with the guys.

And I look cool doin' it all!!! You know it!

Place of Origin:	West Africa
Powers and Skills:	Ability to shape-shift into any animal, enhanced senses
Specialty:	Sniffing out trouble
Favorite Food:	Anything and everything vegetarian, especially tofu, bean burritos, and pie!
Fashion Sense:	Stylin'—or so he thinks

Yo! Hope your summer is super fly! And I ain't lion! —Beast Boy

THE FLASH

The Flash is the Fastest Teenager Alive! He attends Super Hero High to hone his crime-fighting and forensics skills, as well as to master his fleet-footed running abilities. As a member of the Junior Detective Society, The Flash follows his hunches at super-speed. He's trying to learn how to slow down and smell the roses . . . at only half the speed of light.

Place of Origin:	Central City
Powers and Skills:	Super-speed, vibrating his molecules through walls, and detective skills
Specialty:	Getting there quick
Favorite Food:	Fast food!
Fashion Sense:	Aerodynamic and flashy

GREEN LANTERN

Green Lantern is athletic, popular, cool, confident, charismatic, and a Heroball superstar. As a junior member of the Green Lantern Corps, he's in training to protect Earth and the rest of space sector 2814 after he graduates from Super Hero High.

Place of Origin:	Coast City
Powers and Skills:	Flight; the ability to create hard light constructs, force fields, and green energy blasts
Weapon:	Green Lantern power ring
Specialty:	Being fearless
Favorite Food:	Green Arrow's homemade chili
Fashion Sense:	Casual, always with at least a hint of green

SS+GL

SEE YOU AROUND
CAPES & COWLS
-GL

35

THUNDER & LIGHTNING

Thunder and Lightning are sisters with the powers of the elements at their fingertips. Their father is the electrifying super hero known as Black Lightning, and they're quickly following in his footsteps. The sisters share an uncommonly strong bond. Their powers are at their height when they work together.

THUNDER

HOPE your summer ROCKS!! —Thunder

Place of Origin:	Metropolis
Powers and Skills:	Creates powerful, thunderous shock waves
Specialty:	Quick thinking
Favorite Food:	Beans and rice
Fashion Sense:	Loud and proud

LIGHTNING

Hope your summer is
ELECTRIFYING!
— Lightning

Place of Origin:	Metropolis
Powers and Skills:	Generates bolts of lightning
Specialty:	Manipulating and overloading electronics and electrical devices
Favorite Food:	Rice and beans
Fashion Sense:	Bright and sporty

STUDENT LIFE
There's always something super going on!

ADAM STRANGE

As a human who spent time on the planet Rann in the Alpha Centauri galaxy, Adam has come to Super Hero High with his jetpack to achieve new heights of heroic perfection. He is an ace flyer, and pretty normal for a guy named Strange.

Reach for the stars!
—a.s.

Place of Origin:	Earth
Powers and Skills:	Uses alien technology for offense and defense
Weapon:	Jetpack
Favorite Food:	Moon cakes
Fashion Sense:	Space-age

ANIMAL MAN

A healthy dose of alien radiation gave Animal Man the ability to temporarily take on the abilities of any animal. He uses his skills to help others and raise awareness of environmental issues, especially where his friends in the animal kingdom are concerned.

Place of Origin:	San Diego
Powers and Skills:	Takes on the speed, strength, and enhanced senses of different animals
Specialty:	Tracking down trouble
Favorite Food:	Leafy greens
Fashion Sense:	Clothing made of any synthetic material

ARROWETTE

Following in her famous mother's footsteps, this young archer always hits the mark when she aims for justice. Her favorite hero is Green Arrow, but her crime-fighting style is all her own.

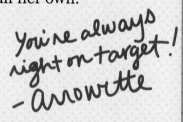

You're always right on target!
— Arrowette

Place of Origin:	Star City
Powers and Skills:	Archery, martial arts
Weapon:	Longbow
Favorite Food:	Apples
Fashion Sense:	Anything athletic makes her quiver

BIG BARDA

Big Barda is a transfer student from Apokolips Magnet, where she majored in evil with Granny Goodness's Female Furies. Big Barda has put those bad days behind her and embraced the hero lifestyle. Some students still believe the saying "Once a villain, always a villain," but Barda is determined to prove them wrong.

Place of Origin:	The planet Apokolips
Powers and Skills:	Super-strength and stamina, extensive hand-to-hand combat training
Weapon:	Mega Rod
Favorite Food:	Mashed potatoes
Fashion Sense:	Operatic and armored

43

CYBORG

BOOYAH!! —C

Cyborg is part man, part machine. His cybernetics always keep him connected to the Internet, so he breezes through his studies with plenty of time for his favorite extracurricular activities, such as playing video games, watching TV, and eating pizza. He only has to worry when his computerized brain gets poor Wi-Fi reception!

Place of Origin:	Detroit
Powers and Skills:	Enhanced intelligence and super-strength
Weapons:	Cybernetic armor and transforming blaster arm
Specialty:	Computer interface abilities
Favorite Food:	Burgers and pizza
Fashion Sense:	Metallic

ELASTI-GIRL

As a child, Elasti-Girl was exposed to mysterious gases from deep within the earth. Now she attends Super Hero High in an attempt to gain mastery over her amazing ability to change size—she can stretch from the size of a tiny mouse to the height of a towering skyscraper.

Place of Origin:	Hollywood
Powers and Skills:	Can grow or shrink her body to extreme sizes
Specialty:	Overshadowing her opponents
Favorite Food:	A tall stack of pancakes
Fashion Sense:	Stretchable

EL DIABLO

Because he's usually calm, cool, and collected, few students would suspect the hothead lurking just beneath El Diablo's easygoing exterior. He is extremely loyal to his friends, and he won't hesitate to use his powers to turn up the heat on any villain who threatens them.

Place of Origin:	Gotham City
Powers and Skills:	Projects fiery plasma from his hands
Specialty:	Heating things up!
Favorite Food:	Salsa—extra, extra, extra hot and spicy
Fashion Sense:	Cool and comfortable

COOL IT, SNOWFLAKE! —FROST

A laboratory accident gave Frost the ability to freeze anything she touches and to generate intense blasts of cold. Unfortunately, she must feed off heat energy to power her wintry ways. While it may seem like Frost has an icy personality, she actually keeps her distance so that she doesn't steal her friends' body heat.

Place of Origin: New York

Powers and Skills: Heat absorption, the creation of ice constructs, brilliant chemist

Specialty: Can freeze anything with a single touch

Favorite Food: Frozen yogurt

Fashion Sense: Winter wear year-round

LADY SHIVA

Only Barda gets away with calling me "SHEEVES"!
Lady Shiva

Lady Shiva prides herself on the discipline that's made her one of the top martial artists at Super Hero High. She likes to keep her brain and body functioning optimally. She always has your back if she considers you a friend.

Place of Origin:	China
Powers and Skills:	Master of martial arts
Specialty:	Perfectly placed kicks
Favorite Food:	Red bean dumplings
Fashion Sense:	Traditional but functional

MISS MARTIAN

Miss Martian is a shy but incredibly powerful shape-shifting alien with psionic powers. Even though she has the ability to read minds, she usually refrains because it's impolite to listen to what other people are thinking. She loves music and hopes to one day share her songs with the world—if only she can get over her stage fright.

Hi.
-M.M.

Place of Origin:	The planet Mars
Powers and Skills:	Flight, shape-shifting, mind reading, invisibility, super-strength, and intangibility
Specialty:	Master of disguise and camouflage
Favorite Food:	Marshmallow cream chocolate cookies
Fashion Sense:	Subtle and unassuming

RAVAGER

Keep your eye on the prize!
—Ravager

With her dramatic flair and drop-dead demeanor, Ravager is the reigning queen of the theater department. If anyone threatens her star status, Ravager's explosive temper comes out. Even though she wears an eye patch, she can see trouble coming from a mile away.

Place of Origin:	Chicago
Powers and Skills:	Advanced hand-to-hand combat
Weapon:	Double swords
Favorite Food:	Kimchi tacos with green apple shavings and sweet peppers
Fashion Sense:	Bold and dramatic

SHAZAM

Have a BLAST! SHAZAM

Deriving her magical power from a number of ancient mythological deities, Shazam may be petite, but she packs a mighty punch! She could end up being one of Super Hero High's greatest graduates one day.

Place of Origin:	Fawcett City
Powers and Skills:	Super-strength, super-speed, flight, intelligence, and the ability to harness and wield lightning
Specialty:	Potential to access almost unlimited power
Favorite Food:	Falafel and hummus
Fashion Sense:	Classic and athletic with a touch of preppy

SILVER BANSHEE

PLAY it LOUD! –SB

Silver Banshee wants to be heard, and her powers of sonic manipulation make it easy. She's also a formidable member of the Debate Team and an epic vocalist with a taste for loud rock in Band Club!

Place of Origin:	Ireland
Powers and Skills:	Sound manipulation
Specialty:	A super-loud sonic scream that she calls the Death Wail
Favorite Food:	Popcorn
Fashion Sense:	Gothic and glamorous

STARFIRE

I hope you have the summer of best-ness and also that it's the greatest.
Yours in the fun-ship,
Starfire

Starfire is a warrior princess from another planet, but despite her exotic alien beauty, she is a down-to-earth girl. She sees the good in everyone, and her kindhearted disposition often brings out the best in her friends. She has a bit of a sibling rivalry with her sister Blackfire, who attends Korugar Academy, where she is more interested in improving her superpower skills than in getting to know her sister.

Place of Origin:	The planet Tamaran
Powers and Skills:	Flight, super-strength, and some degree of invulnerability
Weapon:	Projects energy blasts, known as starbolts, from her hands
Favorite Food:	Ice cream
Fashion Sense:	Exotic and trendy

VIBE

Feel the VIBRATIONS this summer!
—THE BIG V

Never quite here and never quite there, Vibe vibrates between different frequencies to throw his opponents off balance. He excels in both Super Suit Design and Forensics, and he dreams of one day becoming a member of the Justice League of America.

Place of Origin:	Detroit
Powers and Skills:	Creates powerful waves of sonic vibrations, enhanced agility
Specialty:	Emits shock waves from his hands
Favorite Food:	Energy drinks
Fashion Sense:	Fun, funky, and streetwise

The Three **POW**s of Super Hero High

Brain **POW**ers

Super **POW**ers

Will **POW**ers

Another Amazing Year!

First Day of the Semester

Autumn Band Club
Performance

Passing Flyers' Ed with Flying Colors!

First Place Again!

Amanda "The Wall" Waller, Principal

Principal Waller is the hard-nosed, strict, no-nonsense head of Super Hero High. She knows the world can be tough on Supers, and she strives to ensure that her students are ready to take on anything.

You're a one-of-a-kind catch for Super Hero High! Thanks for your hard work and dedication. —Principal Waller

Gorilla Grodd, Vice Principal

Gruff and short-tempered, Grodd is a former super-villain who likes keeping the students in line. He oversees detention and hands out generous sentences to anyone who crosses him.

GET TO CLASS! —GRODD

Lucius Fox, Weaponomics

Anything can be a weapon, from a pencil to a thermonuclear dark matter oscillator, and young Supers learn how to use—and defend *against*—all of them in Mr. Fox's class.

Red Tornado, Flyers' Ed

It takes a levelheaded and unemotional android to teach a group of teenagers how to fly, and Red Tornado does it year after year with style. Passing his intense aerial obstacle course is a point of pride for students.

Crazy Quilt, Super Suit Design

Eccentric, over-the-top, and always entertaining, Crazy Quilt's Super Suit Design class is one of the most popular and important at Super Hero High. Whatever the mission, Crazy Quilt knows the right accessory for it.

Doc Magnus, Robotics and Technology

Doc Magnus is a technological genius with a special talent for building robots. His savvy and easygoing demeanor make his class a hit, especially with the tech-minded students like Cyborg, Bumblebee, and Batgirl.

Wildcat, Phys Ed

A born fighter, Wildcat teaches the fine art of hand-to-hand combat and how to overcome any obstacle by unleashing each student's unique set of superpowers.

June Moon, Art

The hip art teacher who enchants all her students, June Moon believes that unleashing your creative side is as potent as any superpower.

Commissioner Gordon, Forensics, Law Enforcement, and You

Students learn the fundamentals of good sleuthing and solid detective work from one of Gotham City's finest, Police Commissioner Gordon of the Gotham City Police Department.

Parasite, Janitor

Students make a lot of messes, and Parasite is there to take care of every single one of them. He often asks himself, "If they're so super, why can't they clean up after themselves?"

Weaponomics

Your mind is your most powerful weapon.

Mace

Net Gun

Mallet

History

Learn from history. Don't repeat it.

Science
Better crime fighting through science!

1st Place
Gotham City
Science Fair:
Frost

Physical Education

Battle Strategy

Heroic Stances

Heroball Practice

Super Suit Design
Creativity, Craftsmanship, and Practicality

Katana's A+ design
for this year's
Heroball uniforms!

Super Suit Successes . . . or Failures?

SUPERLATIVES

Most Likely to Save the Day:

TIE: Wonder Woman and Bumblebee

Most Fashionable: Katana

Best Student ID Picture: Poison Ivy

Worst Student ID Picture: The Flash

Best Weapons Wielder: Hawkgirl

World's Finest Team:

Supergirl and Batgirl

Best Super Suit: Bumblebee

69

SUPERLATIVES

Most Dynamic Duo:
Harley Quinn and Wonder Woman

Bluntest Bludgeon:
Big Barda and her Mega Rod

Sweetest Smile: Starfire

Most Disciplined: Lady Shiva

Handsomest Hero: Green Lantern

Most Flexible: Elasti-Girl

SUPERLATIVES

Most Dramatic: Star Sapphire

Most Likely to Create Mischief:

Catwoman

Class Clown: Harley Quinn

Most Ferociously Fashionable: Cheetah

SUPERLATIVES

Most Animal Magnetism: BEAST BOY!

—You know it!

Here are a few of the many forms of our favorite wild guy!

What a Croc!
— B.B.

Neatest Room: Bumblebee

Bumblebee's room is neat and sweet as honey.

Messiest Room: Harley Quinn

Harley proves that comedy isn't pretty . . . or tidy.

Coolest Cave: Batgirl

Batgirl's high-tech room has a hint of glamour.

Room That Only Star Sapphire Could Love:

Star Sapphire
Pink! Purple!
Red! Violet!
We can't look any longer!

It is beautiful, isn't it? ♥SS

SCHOOL CLUBS

Junior Detective Society of Metropolis

Do you like solving crimes?

Join the Junior Detective Society!

Meetings held in top-secret location.

All who can find us are welcome.

Current members: Batgirl, Hawkgirl, The Flash, Bumblebee

Vehicles Club

Flyers and non-flyers alike love the roar of an engine and the wind in their hair.

Current members: Batgirl, Harley Quinn, Supergirl, Wonder Woman

Science Club

Put your goggles on as we prepare for explosive fun in the Science Club.

Current members: Ivy, Frost, Star Sapphire, Lightning, and Green Lantern

Model UP (United Planets)

Represent your planet at the Model UP!

Current members: Wonder Woman, Supergirl, Miss Martian, Starfire, Adam Strange, and Big Barda

Wonder Woman must use her diplomatic skills when dealing with Cheetah.

The Furies fail to understand diplomacy.

Track Team

Run, don't walk, to track team tryouts!

Current members: Wonder Woman, Supergirl, The Flash, Animal Man, and Cheetah

Glee Club

Sing out LOUD! (Not so loud, please, Miss Banshee.)

Current members: Miss Martian, Silver Banshee, and Bumblebee

School Internet Radio Station

Cut through the static and join the radio club!

Current members: Bumblebee (night DJ), Star Sapphire (relationship advice guru), and Harley Quinn (sanity checks)

CHESS (Citizens Helping Extraterrestrials Succeed Society)

Be paired with an alien buddy to help them adjust to life on Earth.

Current CHESS buddies: Batgirl and Supergirl;
Bumblebee and Miss Martian;
Lady Shiva and Big Barda;
Wonder Woman and Starfire

Band Club

Feel the beat in your feet—or paws, or tentacles, or whatever.

Current members: Katana, Beast Boy, Silver Banshee,
and Cheetah

HARLEY'S QUINNTESSENTIALS

Harley Quinn shares the fun and funny of Super Hero High School on her show, "Harley's Quinntessentials."

HEROES OF THE MONTH

Looking to see you here next year!

HERO OF THE YEAR

Bumblebee

Bumblebee proves that sometimes the smallest heroes can make the biggest difference!

RIVAL SCHOOLS

APOKOLIPS MAGNET

If constantly plotting to take over Earth counts as higher education, then the Female Furies of Apokolips definitely count as a school rival!

Headmaster:
GRANNY GOODNESS

Mascot:
PERRY THE PARADEMON

Granny Goodness in her harmless librarian disguise

THE FURIES

MAD HARRIET
Powers and Skills:
Sharp claws, earsplitting cackle

LASHINA
Powers and Skills:
Master of electrified metal
bands that she uses as whips

STOMPA
Powers and Skills:
Creates earthquakes
by stomping on the ground

SPEED QUEEN
Powers and Skills:
Expert skater, extreme speed

ARTEMIZ
Powers and Skills:
Amazing archer

RIVAL SCHOOLS

KORUGAR ACADEMY

Korugar Academy attracts some of the
most powerful beings in the universe.
Unfortunately, the curriculum focuses on
individual perfection rather than
on helping others.

Headmaster: SINESTRO

BLACKFIRE

Powers and Skills:

Flight, super-strength, some degree of invulnerability, and the ability to project energy blasts from her hands

Is not my sister the pretty? —Starfire

BLEEZ

Powers and Skills:

Flight; the ability to create hard light constructs, force fields, and energy blasts using her Red Lantern ring

LOBO

Powers and Skills:

Super-strength, super-speed, and regeneration

MAXIMA

Powers and Skills:

Super-strength, super-speed, and the ability to create force fields

MONGAL

Powers and Skills:

Superhuman stamina and energy blast projection

89

THWARTED VILLAINS

GIGANTA

She may be large, but the smallest things set her off. Giganta is currently doing community service to pay for her crimes.

CROC

Lurking in the sewers of Metropolis, Croc is always on the hunt for his next meaty meal. Bumblebee and Beast Boy curbed his cravings when they took him down.

THWARTED VILLAINS

KING SHARK

He came from the depths of the ocean and had big plans for taking over Metropolis. Luckily, Bumblebee's tech and Harley's mallet defeated this oversized fish.

Belle Reve Penitentiary and Juvenile Detention Center: incarcerating SUPER-VILLAINS for over one hundred years!

LION MANE

Wielding power over animals, Lion Mane tried to unleash an animal army on the city, but Hawkgirl made sure justice was served!

All in a day's work!
—Hawkgirl

SOLOMON GRUNDY

This zombie monster terrorized Metropolis, but thanks to the students at Super Hero High, he now rests peacefully behind bars.

METROPOLIS BANK

PROUD SUPPORTER OF SUPER HERO HIGH SCHOOL!

COME IN FOR OUR

"SAVING THE DAY"

SPECIAL AND GET A FREE SMOOTHIE BLENDER

WHEN YOU OPEN A SAVINGS ACCOUNT!

Eclipso Jewels

Super Hero High students,
you make us sparkle!

As the finest jeweler in Metropolis,
we get robbed again and again and again!
And you are always there to save us!

Thank you!

Capes & Cowls Café
Is Now Serving:

Tamaran Gorka Berry Pie

Honey Smoothies

Apokoliptian Fire Chili

Krypton Krispies

Superfood Cake (available in Quinoa, Cauliflower, or Spinach)

Bean Burritos

Soder™ Cola

Favorite Off-Campus Friend:
Steve Trevor

I'd like to thank
the Super Hero High
students for their efforts in
saving the café from
52 robberies, 13 super-villain
takeovers, 3 giant attacks,
and one scary spider.

—Steve Trevor